UNICORN ACADEMY

...Where magic happens!

Lily and Feather

JULIE SYKES

illustrated by
LUCY TRUMAN

nosy crow

To the Quornicorns Pony Club Quiz Team
- Cleo, Mia, Libby and Iola -
you are all absolute stars!

First published in the UK in 2020 by Nosy Crow Ltd
The Crow's Nest, 14 Baden Place
Crosby Row, London, SE1 1YW

www.nosycrow.com

ISBN: 978 1 78800 923 2

Nosy Crow and associated logos are trademarks
and/or registered trademarks of Nosy Crow Ltd.

Text copyright © Julie Sykes and Linda Chapman, 2020
Illustrations copyright © Lucy Truman, 2020
Cover typography © Joel Holland, 2020

A CIP catalogue record for this book is available from the British Library.

Printed and bound in Great Britain by Clays Ltd, Elcograf S.p.A.

Papers used by Nosy Crow are made from
wood grown in sustainable forests.

MIX
Paper from
responsible sources
FSC® C018072
FSC
www.fsc.org

3 5 7 9 10 8 6 4 2

CHAPTER ONE

"Here we are, Lils," Lily's mum said. "Unicorn Academy – your home for the next year!"

"Oh, wow!" Lily's breath rushed out as she stared up at the enormous glass and marble building. On the top of the tallest tower, a pink flag with a white unicorn on it was rippling in the breeze. "It's beautiful," she said, looking at the gardens bursting with winter plants and flowers and the multicoloured lake shimmering in the distance.

Her mother smiled. "It is, isn't it? It hasn't changed one bit since I was here. You're going to

have such a fantastic time. I just know it!"

Lily couldn't speak. Her tummy felt like it was tying itself in knots. She'd wanted to come to Unicorn Academy for ages – she had been longing to be paired with a unicorn and to start training to become a guardian of beautiful Unicorn Island. However, now she was here, and the academy looked so big and grand, she was beginning to wonder whether her invitation to become a student there had been a mistake. The other new students all looked so confident as they chattered to each other and waved their parents goodbye.

What if I'm not good enough to be a guardian? Lily thought, with a rush of panic. *What if I mess things up and get asked to leave? Mum will be so disappointed.*

A teacher bustled up. She wore her brown hair in a neat bun held in place with silver clips. Three girls were following her, clutching overnight bags.

"Hello, I'm Ms Rosemary, I teach Care of

Unicorns, and you are?" the teacher said to Lily.

Lily was feeling so overwhelmed, the words seemed to stick in her throat. "I'm … um … um…" she stammered.

"Lily Jamieson," her mum put in.

Ms Rosemary looked at her clipboard. "That's handy! Lily, you're going to be in Amethyst dorm with these three. This is Aisha." She pointed to a girl who was carrying a flute case and had curly black hair in a high ponytail. The girl grinned at Lily, who smiled shyly back.

"And this is Zara," Ms Rosemary continued. Zara had dark brown hair that stopped just past her shoulders and intelligent green eyes that slanted upwards. She studied Lily for a moment and then gave her a smile.

"And Phoebe," Ms Rosemary finished. Phoebe was tall and slim, with honey-blonde hair in two waist-length plaits. She beamed.

"Hi, Lily! Isn't this super-awesome!" She swept her arms out dramatically. "I mean, look around.

It's gorgeous, isn't it? We're just soooooo lucky to have been invited to be students here!"

Lily thought it sounded like everything Phoebe said should have an exclamation mark after it.

"Say goodbye to your mum, Lily," said Ms Rosemary. "Then we need to get to the hall. It's almost time for the ceremony where you will be paired with your unicorns."

Lily felt a flutter of delight. She was going to have a unicorn of her own!

Mum stepped forward. "Goodbye, Lils, have a wonderful time. Make sure you write and tell me all your news." She hugged her and then gently pushed her towards Ms Rosemary. "Go on, off you go!"

Torn between excitement at meeting her unicorn, sadness at saying goodbye to her mum, and still feeling like she'd been invited to the academy by mistake, Lily followed Ms Rosemary

and the other girls up the marble steps and through the huge front door into the academy. The entrance hall was vast, with statues of unicorns in the corners and huge oil paintings on the walls.

"No more talking, please," Ms Rosemary said with a warning look at Phoebe, who was chattering to Zara.

As Ms Rosemary ushered them all into the hall, Lily swallowed a gasp. Light shone through the coloured swirls of the domed glass roof, filling the hall with rainbows and illuminating a huge map that was taking pride of place in the centre of the room. Lily craned her neck for a better look. The magical force field that kept the map safe hummed softly as she passed by. Lily's mum had told her it was an exact replica of Unicorn Island and it could transport anyone anywhere on the island. Students and unicorns

were forbidden from using it without Ms Nettles' permission. Lily hoped she'd get to use it at some point.

That's if I'm good enough to stay here, she reminded herself.

"Oh, wow! Look at the unicorns!" Aisha whispered, pointing.

A fresh wave of excitement swept away Lily's anxiety as she followed Aisha's gaze and saw a group of young unicorns standing at the side of the stage. They were beautiful. Their sparkling white coats were covered with different-coloured patterns and their long silky manes and tails were full of colours. Some of them eyed the students boldly but others hung back, peeping out shyly from behind the stage curtains.

"Lily, over here!" Hearing her name, Lily saw that Aisha, Phoebe and Zara had gone on ahead and were now waving her over to a row of seats.

Lily and Feather

But just as Lily stepped towards the spare ones, two other girls barged past. One had bushy brown hair and narrow eyes, the other had red hair in a high ponytail. "Come on, Amber. Let's sit here!" said the brown-haired girl. They plonked themselves in the seats next to Aisha, Phoebe and Zara.

"Excuse me but Lily was about to sit there," said Zara politely.

The two girls gave Lily a challenging look.

"It's OK, I'll sit somewhere else," said Lily quickly. The girls looked scary.

"Oh, please, can't you both sit somewhere else? We'd really like to sit together because we're in the same dorm," Aisha pleaded with them.

"Tough," said the brown-haired girl with a shrug.

"It's fine," Lily said quickly. "I can sit back there." She pointed to a seat in the row behind.

To the Quornicorns Pony Club Quiz Team
- Cleo, Mia, Libby and Iola -
you are all absolute stars!

First published in the UK in 2020 by Nosy Crow Ltd
The Crow's Nest, 14 Baden Place
Crosby Row, London, SE1 1YW

www.nosycrow.com

ISBN: 978 1 78800 923 2

A CIP catalogue record for this book is available from the British Library.

Printed and bound in Great Britain by Clays Ltd, Elcograf S.p.A.

Papers used by Nosy Crow are made from
wood grown in sustainable forests.

3 5 7 9 10 8 6 4 2

each other and looking after Unicorn Island. You will graduate when your unicorn has discovered their magic and when you have bonded with them. You will know when this happens as a lock of your hair will turn the same colour as your unicorn's mane. Some unicorns need a little longer to discover their magic, or to bond, so some of you may need to stay on for a second year in order to graduate."

Ms Nettles seemed to glance in Lily's direction. Lily squirmed in her seat. Did the headteacher suspect she might not graduate? To her relief, Ms Nettles' gaze swept on.

"You will make many friends while you are here but undoubtedly the most important friendship will be the one you form with your unicorn. In December, on the longest night of the year, students and their unicorns will graduate at the magnificent Sparkle Lake Ball! Then you will

return home together as lifelong friends and partners.

But to start this exciting journey you must first be paired with a unicorn." A smile softened her strict face. "Let the pairing ceremony begin!"

CHAPTER TWO

Lily studied the unicorns eagerly. Which one would be hers? Hopefully not the tall unicorn with the silver-blue mane and proud stare. He was very beautiful but looked far too regal to be her partner. She wouldn't know what to say to him! And the smaller unicorn next to him with the red and orange mane looked much too naughty and mischievous. His dark eyes held a very cheeky twinkle. A unicorn with a pretty pink mane shouldered impatiently past him and stamped a hoof, looking confidently out at the audience.

Lily's attention was caught by a unicorn

with a violet, yellow and blue mane who was standing right at the back. She was peeking out shyly from under her silky forelock. Her long eyelashes fluttered as she glanced out at the girls and boys before staring at the floor. Lily's heart melted. The unicorn looked awkward, as if she felt she didn't belong there. *Just like me*, Lily thought.

Ms Nettles began to call out names – the student's first and then the unicorn's. The first pairing was a boy from Topaz dorm called Spike, who had bright-red hair and an impish look, and Dynamo, the mischievous unicorn with the red and orange

mane. They both seemed delighted as they moved to the far side of the stage, immediately putting their matching red heads together and looking as though they were plotting trouble.

One by one, Ms Nettles called out names until it was the turn of Amethyst dorm.

"Aisha," said Ms Nettles. "You will be paired with Silver."

Aisha shimmied from her chair, humming a happy tune. Silver was a small unicorn with a green, silver and red mane. He danced out from the crowd, lifting his glittering hooves high, his tail swishing merrily. Aisha ran up the steps and threw her arms round him straight away. He nuzzled her happily and, hearing the sound of her tune, he trotted in time to it as they walked over to the far side of the stage.

The watching students giggled.

"Oh dear," said Ms Nettles, shaking her head.

"I hope I haven't made a mistake pairing you two music-lovers together!" She silenced the gigglers with a stern look. "Next from Amethyst dorm we have Phoebe. You will be paired with Shimmer."

Phoebe gave a high-pitched squeal of delight as a flamboyant unicorn with a pink and blue mane that reached to his knees whinnied. "Oh, wow! I was hoping for that exact unicorn! Thank you, Ms Nettles! Thank you! You've made my dreams come true!" She ran up the steps and hugged the headteacher who looked very taken aback.

"That will do, my dear!" she said, shooing Phoebe away.

"This is the best day of my ENTIRE life, everyone!" Phoebe declared dramatically. She raced over to Shimmer.

"We will be friends for ever!" Shimmer exclaimed with a toss of his luxuriant mane. He seemed just as dramatic as Phoebe.

Lily and Feather

Ms Nettles cleared her throat. "Very nice, dears. Now, move to the side, please."

Rather reluctantly Phoebe and Shimmer left the centre of the stage and joined Aisha and Silver.

Zara was paired with a dreamy-looking unicorn with a silver mane who was called Moonbeam, and then finally it was Lily's turn.

"Lily, you will be paired with…" Lily's heart raced as she stared at the remaining unicorns. Which one was it going to be?

"Feather," Ms Nettles announced.

Lily's heart leapt as the nervous unicorn she'd spotted earlier stepped shyly forward. Feather stumbled awkwardly as she reached the centre of the stage. Lily hurried up the steps, blushing furiously, aware that the whole room was watching them.

"Um … hi," she said.

"Hi," muttered Feather, staring at the floor.

Lily could tell Feather hated being watched by everyone just as much as she did. It made her feel braver, like she wanted to protect her.

"I was hoping you'd be my unicorn," she whispered.

Lily and Feather

Feather's eyes flew to hers and as their gazes met Lily felt a strong connection surge between them. Feather nuzzled her, her warm, sweet-smelling breath tickling Lily's hands.

They joined the others in Amethyst dorm while Ms Nettles moved on to Opal dorm. All around Lily the students who had been paired up were whispering excitedly to their unicorns. She and Feather exchanged shy looks.

Skye and Amber, the two girls who had been mean to Lily, were in Opal dorm and were the last to be paired up with their unicorns.

Skye was given a sweet-looking unicorn called Firefly, and Amber was paired with Swift, the impatient unicorn with the pink mane. The noise level rose.

Ms Nettles clapped her hands for silence and surveyed the pairs. "You now have the rest of the afternoon before tea to get to know your unicorn.

Make the most of this free time. Lessons will start tomorrow. Timetables will be in your bedroom when you go to unpack."

"Where would you like to go first?" Lily asked Feather as they all filed out of the back door of the hall that led directly into the gardens.

"I don't mind," Feather whispered.

"I don't mind either," said Lily.

Skye and Amber were passing by.

"I don't mind. I don't mind either," mimicked Skye, in perfect imitation of Feather and Lily's voices.

Amber giggled. "Listen, Skye, Lily's squeaking like a tiny mouse again."

Feather glared at them.

"What are you doing here?" Skye said, looking Lily up and down. "You're such a little mouse. The teachers must have made a mistake inviting you to train at Unicorn Academy."

Lily's heart clenched, her eyes glistening with

tears, as Skye casually spoke her greatest fear out loud. Luckily Skye was already looking round for the next thing to do and didn't see. "Come on, Amber, let's find our dorm and go exploring!" she said, vaulting on to Firefly and trotting away.

Amber leapt on Swift and cantered after her.

Lily blinked, trying hard not to cry.

Feather nuzzled her. "I don't like that girl. She's mean."

Lily felt a little better.

"Hey, Lily!"

Hearing Zara's voice, Lily swung round. The rest of her dorm were beckoning her over. "We thought we'd ride round the grounds together so we can get to know each other as we explore," said Zara. "Do you and Feather want to join in?"

What Lily really wanted was to go somewhere on her own with Feather, but she didn't want her dorm to think she was unfriendly. She swallowed

the hard lump in her throat. "OK. Thanks," she managed to say and, jumping on to Feather, she joined the others.

"We should dip our hands in Sparkle Lake as we look round," said Aisha. "My dad said it's a tradition on your first day here."

Lily's mum had told her that too. She was just about to tell the others that but she was too late – Zara had started talking.

"Did you know that all the magic water that flows around the island comes from Sparkle Lake? It rises up from the centre of the earth through the fountain in the middle of the lake and then it's carried around the island in rivers and streams."

"I really want to see it!" said Phoebe.

"Then what are we waiting for?" said Zara. "Let's go!"

As Lily explored with the others, she tried to push Skye's words to the back of her mind. They

rode to the glittering lake then on to the play park, through the neat vegetable garden and orchard, then down to the stream that ran through the lush meadows.

I love it here, Lily thought, her heart filling with delight. *I want to learn how to protect the school and the island. I'm going to try really hard in all my lessons. Oh, please let Skye be wrong and let me be good enough to stay.*

They reached the cross-country course. Lily looked eagerly at it. She had a pony back at home and she often took him jumping. She couldn't wait to have a go on Feather, although there was a sign up saying they mustn't jump without a teacher present. "I love cross-country," she said.

"Me too!" said Zara.

"Look at those jumps!" Phoebe squealed. "They're huge! Have you ever done fences like that?" She didn't wait for them to answer. "I did once. I was riding my sister's horse back at home

and he just took off with me and galloped towards a ginormous hedge. I was sure I was going to die but thankfully I managed to stay on."

"It looks like Topaz dorm have been here before us," Zara said, riding up to a big log pile and studying it. "Spike and Dynamo ignored the notice and jumped this fence."

Lily wondered how she could possibly know that. Phoebe clearly had the same thought. "How can you tell?" she asked curiously.

"Look," said Zara. "There are four sets of hoof prints leading up to the jump. Topaz dorm is the only other dorm with four people in it so it must have been them. There's only one set of hoof prints leading away from the jump and the hooves have a distinct oval shape. I noticed Dynamo's hooves were shaped like that when Spike was paired with him so that suggests it was Dynamo who jumped it. The final clue, well, look

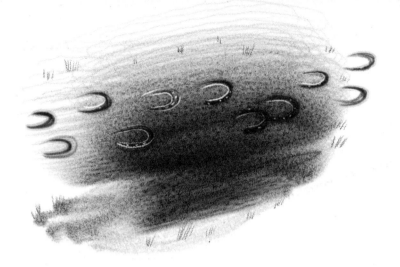

over there!" She pointed to the jump.

Even Aisha had stopped humming to listen. "What are we looking at?" she said, bewildered.

"Don't you see the red and orange hairs caught on the wood? They must have snagged there as a unicorn jumped over." Zara rode Moonbeam over. "Dynamo is the only unicorn in Topaz dorm to have a red and orange mane so it must have been him."

"That's so cool!" said Phoebe, her eyes wide.

"You're just like a detective, Zara!" agreed Aisha.

Lily nodded hard, feeling very impressed.

Zara grinned. "I love solving mysteries and while I'm here at the academy I intend to solve any that come our way!"

Lily and Feather

Lily forced herself to speak up. "My mum said that lots of mysterious things happened here last year."

"Yes, I heard that," said Zara. "Someone was trying to harm all the unicorns."

"It was the school nurse, Ms Willow," said Phoebe. "She was trying to poison them all with one of her special tonics! Most of the unicorns almost died!"

"No, they didn't," said Zara. "Honestly, Phoebe, if you keep exaggerating and making stuff up, then no one will believe you when you are telling the truth. Ms Willow never tried to poison anyone. She wanted to bind all the unicorns to her so that they had to do what she said. She almost succeeded. The year before that, the old headteacher – Ms Primrose – turned bad and tried to sabotage the whole school."

Aisha's eyes gleamed. "Oh, I hope something

exciting happens while we're here. Imagine how much fun it would be to have a mystery to solve."

Lily grinned. It did sound exciting.

"We must keep our eyes peeled!" Phoebe declared. "If any mystery comes along, we'll work it out!"

"Definitely," said Zara. "Amethyst dorm is the best. We'll always save the day!"

The unicorns whinnied as the four new friends cheered.

CHAPTER THREE

Lily's first few days at the academy flew by. There was so much to do – teachers to meet, stable routines to work out, names to learn and lessons to start. Lily concentrated really hard in all her lessons, not wanting to give the teachers any excuse to be unhappy with her. She didn't like putting her hand up in class because she hated it when everyone looked at her but she tried to make up for being quiet by putting lots of effort into her work. She was so tired at the end of each day that she fell asleep the minute she got into bed.

"Can you believe we've been at the academy for three days?" she said to Feather on the fourth morning as she got her ready for their first lesson of the day – Care of Unicorns with Ms Rosemary. Lily already thought of Feather as her best friend. She could talk to her about anything without feeling awkward or worrying about what Feather would think of her.

"It's gone really fast," Feather agreed. "But…"

"But what?' Lily prompted, lifting a strand of mane to comb it out.

"I really like it here but I still don't really know the other unicorns very well. They all act like they've known each other for ever."

"I feel like that too," Lily admitted. "Zara, Aisha and Phoebe talk all the time, whereas often I don't know what to say so I usually don't say anything at all. I really like them but I bet they all think I'm boring."

"No one could think that!" said Feather indignantly.

Lily smiled. "Thanks. I wish I could just speak out more…" She broke off as Phoebe, Zara and Aisha arrived in the stables with a group of other students.

Phoebe pointed dramatically at Lily. "It's Lily! She's safe!"

Lily blinked. "What?"

Phoebe waved a crumpled piece of paper with Lily's name in the corner. "I found this in the dorm when we got up. You seemed to have disappeared. We were sure that you'd been kidnapped and you were trying to write us a note before you were whisked away."

"Actually, it was *Phoebe* who was sure you'd been kidnapped," Zara put in, with a sigh. "I was pretty sure you'd be here. You always get up early, before the rest of us, your boots and coat had gone and I

noticed that you'd taken the roll of plaiting ribbon that had been on your bedside table."

"So *is* this yours?" Phoebe held out the piece of paper to Lily.

"Yes, I meant to throw it in the bin but I must have missed," said Lily, stuffing the paper in a pocket. She loved folding paper into shapes and she'd been trying to make a unicorn but it hadn't gone very well and so she'd screwed it up.

"It was just a bit of scrap paper, like Zara said. You're such a drama queen, Phoebs," said Aisha, shaking her head.

"I might have been right," said Phoebe, unabashed. "Lily might have been kidnapped.

"Lily? Kidnapped?" Skye scoffed to Amber as they walked past. "Who'd want to kidnap quiet little Lily mouse! She'd bore her kidnappers to death!"

"Yeah," Amber agreed. "I bet the teachers

wouldn't even notice she was gone, she's so quiet."

They giggled together as they went to get their grooming kits.

Lily tipped her head forward so a wing of hair hid her embarrassment. The last thing she wanted was for Skye and Amber to look back and start squeaking at her. It was bad enough when they called her Lily mouse.

"Ignore them," said Aisha, glaring after Skye and Amber.

Lily nodded. She knew that was the best thing to do but it was easier said than done.

Ms Rosemary arrived carrying a big box of coloured ribbons. "Morning, everyone. As I told you yesterday, we're going to be practising plaiting today. I'm going to demonstrate on my unicorn, Blossom. Please make your way outside now with your unicorns and bring your grooming kits."

Lily and Feather hung back as everyone jostled to go outside, tagging along at the back as the students and unicorns formed a large circle around Blossom.

"Before you can start plaiting, you need to comb your unicorn's mane out with either of these," said Ms Rosemary, holding up a metal comb and a soft brush. "You start by sectioning the mane into small pieces, like this." As Ms Rosemary began demonstrating on Blossom's golden mane, Ms Nettles appeared and beckoned her over.

The two teachers broke off to talk in hushed whispers, glancing towards Lily and Feather.

"Lily, they seem to be looking at us," said Feather uneasily.

"I know." Lily felt anxious as she watched Ms Rosemary and Ms Nettles glance at them again. *Had Ms Nettles realised she'd made a mistake in inviting her to train as a guardian? Had she heard how quiet she was in class? Was she going to send her home?* Her heart sped up as Ms Nettles approached her.

Ms Nettles smiled kindly. "Lily dear, I'd like to have a little chat. It won't take long."

Lily could feel everyone's eyes on her as she followed Ms Nettles over to a drinking trough in a quiet corner of the yard. Her heart was now banging like a drum.

Ms Nettles turned to face her.

"Please don't send me home!" The words burst out of Lily before Ms Nettles could speak. "Please, Ms Nettles! I really want to be a guardian. I don't want to leave! I'll try really hard to speak more."

Ms Nettles blinked in surprise. "Leave? Whatever are you talking about, Lily?"

"I… I…" Lily stuttered as she began to feel she might have got the wrong end of the stick. "I thought you were about to say that you'd made a mistake by inviting me to be a student here."

Ms Nettles usually stern gaze softened. "I most certainly was not about to say that. Your teachers have all told me how pleased they are with you. They say you are one of our hardest-working students. Why ever would I want to send you home?"

Lily looked at the floor.

Ms Nettles regarded her for a moment. "You are certainly not about to be sent home and I definitely have not made a mistake. Guardians all have different strengths, just as unicorns have different magic powers. I hope you will discover your own strengths while you are here. Now, the

Lily and Feather

reason I need to talk to you is about your mother."

Lily's felt a rush of anxiety. "Is she OK?"

"Yes. She phoned me this morning because she wanted you to know that she's moving in with your Auntie Louise for a bit. There was a freak weather event in your village last night; it was hit by a tornado. A purple one. It destroyed many of the buildings."

Lily's hands flew to her mouth. "Oh, no! Was anyone hurt?"

Ms Nettles shook her head. "Thankfully not. However, some of the houses, including your own, will need to be rebuilt. The tornado was very strong."

"That's awful!" said Lily. She sniffed, suddenly feeling very homesick and wishing that she was back in her village so that she could check up on everyone. "And really strange – we've never had a tornado in my village before." Her village was on the east coast of the island and sheltered by a range of mountains. It was very rare for them to have bad weather of any kind.

"It is extremely unusual," agreed Ms Nettles. "Luckily, as I say, there were no injuries."

Lily nodded.

Feather's dark eyes were full of concern as Lily rejoined the lesson. "Is everything all right?"

In whispers, Lily told Feather what had happened.

Feather rubbed her head against Lily's arm. "How scary. Your poor mum. It sounds like she had a lucky escape."

"I know. I wish I could see her and give her

a hug." Lily thought of the piece of crumpled paper in her pocket. As soon as the lesson was over, she'd smooth the paper out and fold it into a dove, her mother's favourite bird, and send it to her.

Aisha, Zara and Phoebe came over. "What did Ms Nettles want?" Aisha whispered, glancing at Ms Rosemary, who was patiently explaining plaiting all over again to the boys in Topaz dorm.

"It must have been serious," said Zara, searching Lily's face for clues.

"Oh my gosh! Are you in trouble?" Phoebe gasped.

Skye overheard and snorted with laughter. "Lily in trouble? As if! Lily's scared of her own shadow!"

"No she's not!" Feather stamped a hoof furiously. "Leave Lily alone, Skye!" A pink spark flickered in the corner of Lily's eye and she

caught the scent of something sweet.

"Or what?" Skye laughed.

"Or… Or I'll get really cross!" Feather glared at

her even though Lily could see her body trembling with nerves.

Skye grinned. "Ooh, I'm so scared, Feather!" she teased.

"Ssh! Ms Rosemary's coming," said Firefly quickly. "Skye, you haven't finished plaiting my mane!"

"What's going on here?" Ms Rosemary said, walking over.

No one said anything.

"Hmm," said Ms Rosemary, looking round at them all. "Well, judging by the look of these plaits, none of you should be standing chit-chatting. You've all got some practising to do unless you want me to keep you back for an extra plaiting class at lunchtime."

There were squeaks of alarm and everyone moved quickly away. Lily hugged Feather, her black hair mingling with Feather's violet, yellow

and blue mane.

"Thank you for standing up for me," she whispered.

"It was nothing," mumbled Feather modestly.

But Lily knew exactly how much courage it had taken and she felt a rush of love for her loyal unicorn. "You're the best, Feather. I'm so glad I was paired with you."

Feather whickered softly and rubbed her head against Lily's chest.

CHAPTER FOUR

At dinner time Lily found out she was not the only one with family who'd had been affected by a purple tornado. Reports had come in of other tornadoes that had struck without warning, leaving a trail of damage and a thick layer of purple dust behind as they spun on.

"My aunt on the east coast lost every single tree in her garden," Johan from Topaz dorm announced, twirling a strand of spaghetti round his fork. "One tree landed across her front door. The neighbours had to rescue her."

"My dad was taking a bath when the roof blew

43

right off our house," said Spike. "He said he'd never grabbed a towel so quickly!" There were gales of laughter. Spike grinned and ran a hand through his red hair. "It's true," he added. "And my granny was staying over and her false teeth ended up in the paddock with Franny, the donkey. Mum only just stopped Franny from eating them."

Lily giggled. Sometimes she didn't know who told taller tales – Spike or Phoebe.

"Hmm. I wonder what's causing all these tornadoes." Zara pulled a tiny notebook and pencil from her pocket. She wrote the date at the top of a new page. "It's extremely unusual to have so many all at once. I think we should make notes of where the tornadoes occurred and at what time."

"Wow, I feel so much safer now that Detective Zara is on the case," said Skye sarcastically, rolling her eyes at Amber.

Zara sent Skye a withering glare. "My uncle actually is a detective and I've been learning lots of skills from him."

"*My uncle actually is a detective*," Skye mimicked, sounding remarkably like Zara. "Get over yourself, Zara. The tornadoes are caused by freak weather. The fact there are so many is just a coincidence."

Lily envied the way Zara just shrugged Skye's teasing off. "Laugh all you want, Skye," Zara said. "But my Uncle Tom says a good detective should always be suspicious of coincidences."

"What if these tornadoes are caused by dark magic and they're part of an evil plot to take over the island?" said Phoebe, her eyes widening. "It could be Ms Primrose or Ms Willow again!"

"No it couldn't, they're both in prison," Zara pointed out.

"But it could be someone else! It's a proper mystery!" said Aisha in excitement.

"Oh, pur-lease!" scoffed Skye. "It's just a few tornadoes caused by bad weather. That's all. You lot are so dumb!"

Zara turned her back on Skye. "It *could* just be bad weather conditions," she said to Aisha, Phoebe and Lily. "But I think there may be more to it. I wonder if there's a pattern to these tornadoes?"

Lily had a thought – could the magic map help them? Maybe it would now show the damaged buildings and trees and if they looked at it, they might be able to see if there was a pattern to where the tornadoes were hitting. She was going to suggest it to the others when she hesitated. What if they went to the map and there wasn't any damage marked on it? She'd look really stupid. *Someone else is bound to think about checking the map*, she thought and stayed quiet.

Everyone continued to argue about whether

the tornadoes were part of an evil plan or just freak weather. It began to make Lily's head hurt. Quietly she left the table and ran to the stables. Feather was in her stall picking at a net of hay. She left it immediately, coming over to softly nuzzle Lily's hands.

"Lily, is everything all right?"

"Yes," said Lily, rubbing her forehead. "The others are arguing about all the purple tornadoes that have been hitting the island so I thought I'd come and talk to you instead."

Feather rubbed her muzzle against Lily. "I'm glad you did. I always like seeing you."

She blinked at her. "It makes me feel warm inside."

Lily put an arm round her neck. "I feel like that too. I've never had a best friend before, Feather. I…" She hesitated and then decided to say what she wanted to even if it was a bit embarrassing. "I feel like I have got one now."

"Me?" said Feather uncertainly.

Despite her embarrassment, Lily laughed. "Of course you!" Feather gave a happy sigh. Lily rested her cheek on her neck. For a few moments they just stood there in contented silence.

"I wish we could do something to stop the tornadoes," Lily said. "They sound awful and what if one comes to the school?" She thought of the beautiful building and its grounds being wrecked. It would be dreadful.

"Do you think one might actually come here?" asked Feather anxiously.

"I'm not sure. Zara thinks there might be a pattern. I wonder if we might be able to see one if we look at the magic map." She glanced at Feather, wondering what she would think.

"That's a brilliant idea!" said Feather. "Why don't you go and have a look?"

Lily nodded, feeling pleased. "It's a bit late now. I'll go tomorrow. I might even ask Aisha, Zara and Phoebe to come with me." Feather made her feel so much braver that anything seemed possible when they were together. *Yes*, she told herself firmly. *Tomorrow I'll ask the others to come and look at the magic map with me, and we'll see if we can work out what's going on … and if the academy's in danger!*

CHAPTER FIVE

The next morning, Lily didn't feel so confident about asking the others if they wanted to look at the map with her.

Maybe I should go on my own first, she decided at breakfast as she ate her cereal. *That way, if nothing is showing on the map I won't feel stupid.*

She hung back as Zara, Aisha and Phoebe went back to the dorm to get ready for Geography with Ms Rivers, and then she headed for the hall. As she walked through the entrance hall she saw Skye, Amber and Lorna, another girl from Opal dorm, huddled round a statue of a rearing unicorn.

Lily and Feather

"Go on, I dare you to do it!" hissed Skye.

Lorna giggled as she quickly scrambled on to the unicorn's back. She pulled a pair of frilly pink pants from her pocket and hooked them over the unicorn's head, pulling them this way and that until they sat jauntily over one ear. "What do you think?" she called down to Skye and Amber.

"Wicked!" Rocking with laughter, Skye and Amber gave Lorna the thumbs-up.

Lily stared in disbelief. How could they look so happy, and play silly dares, when there were tornadoes causing devastation around the island, and the school itself might be at risk? Surely it was only a matter of time before someone was badly injured?

"Squeak, squeak! Look, it's little Lily mouse!"

said Skye, noticing her. "Are these your frilly pants, Lily mouse?" She hooted with laughter.

Amber and Lorna joined in, "Squeak, squeak, squeak!" They giggled.

Lily ran past them and didn't stop running until she reached the main hall. The big double doors were slightly ajar. She glanced around. She wasn't planning to use the map – she just wanted to look at it. But what if a teacher found her near it and she got into trouble just for being there without permission?

She made up her mind. It was worth the risk.

Slipping through the doors, she hurried towards the map. The magical force field buzzed softly as if to warn her away. Lily took a deep breath and the butterflies careering behind her ribcage slowed down. Would the force field let her close enough for a proper look? She walked purposefully towards it and as she approached

there was a soft pop and the humming stopped. A grin spread across Lily's face.

"Thanks," she whispered to the map. It was as though it was happy she was there – maybe it even wanted her to help.

The map was even more incredible close up. The glass and marble model of the school looked so real that, peering through a tiny window, Lily almost expected to see herself inside the building!

She looked to the east, to her village. She could see the ruined houses and for a moment it took her breath away – *how awful for everyone*! Her eyes searched across the map, plotting the path of the freak purple tornadoes by following the fallen trees and damaged buildings. The tornadoes clearly seemed to be zigzagging across the island from the east coast to the west and back again. She traced the pattern with her eyes. If it continued in the same way then the tornadoes would definitely reach the school!

Lily jumped as she heard voices outside the doors. Someone was coming! She mustn't be discovered – she could get in trouble. She had to hide!

She hared across the hall, scrambled on to the stage and ducked behind the stage curtains just as Ms Mallow, the new school nurse, came in with Ms Rivers, the teacher who taught both

Lily and Feather

Geography and Culture. Ms Mallow walked towards the map. Lily held her breath, letting it out quietly when she heard the soft hum of the force field again. Ms Mallow shook her head. "Strange, I was sure the force field had stopped working for a moment then but it seems all right. I must have imagined it."

"It was sensible to check, what with everything that's happening," said Ms Rivers. "Now, where's that book I said I'd lend you?" She walked up the steps on to the stage and went to the piano.

Lily froze, hardly daring to breathe as Ms Rivers came within touching distance of her.

"Here it is." Ms Rivers picked the book up and returned to the floor. "Are you sure that I can't persuade you to come to the meeting Ms Nettles is holding at lunchtime, Ms Mallow?"

"No, Ms Nettles has given me special permission to get on with my work," said Ms Mallow. "I'm

making a large batch of cough syrup. You know how it is at the beginning of a winter term. The students spread their germs with the speed of a forest fire and if these tornadoes are being caused by bad magic, we're going to need the students to stay strong and healthy."

Ms Rivers nodded, worry lines creasing her face. "It does seem like these tornadoes might be part of an evil plan. No one has ever heard of a purple tornado on the island before, let alone lots of them."

"But who would create such terrible things?" asked Ms Mallow.

Ms Rivers looked grave. "Someone who uses dark magic and wants to harm our island and the people and unicorns who live on it."

Ms Rivers and Ms Mallow left the hall.

Lily's heart was thumping so hard she felt sure it was about to explode. Still trembling, she came

out from behind the curtain, crept out of the hall and raced up to the dorm. She had to tell the others what she'd seen and overheard!

The girls were getting ready, sorting out their pencil cases and bags. As Lily burst in, they looked round.

"I know something about the tornadoes!" she exclaimed, her usual shyness overcome by the urge to tell them what she'd discovered.

Everyone gaped at her. The words continued to tumble from her mouth as she described how she'd gone to look at the map and overheard the teachers talking.

"The damage is all there on the map and the pattern is very clear," she finished breathlessly. "The tornadoes are criss-crossing up the island from east to west and back again. Ms Rivers thinks someone might have used dark magic to create them, someone who wants to harm the island!"

"But that's terrible!" exclaimed Phoebe.

"Who would want to harm the island?" asked Aisha.

"Ms Rivers didn't seem to know," said Lily.

"I'll write to my Uncle Tom, the detective, and see if he knows of any likely suspects," said Zara. She pulled out her notebook and scribbled a note to herself.

"The worst thing is that, when I was looking at the map, I could see that if the tornadoes keep going in this pattern they're going to reach the academy," Lily said.

"What! The school could be destroyed and our unicorns might be hurt?" cried Phoebe.

Lily nodded anxiously.

"But surely the teachers will stop the tornadoes in time, won't they?" said Aisha.

Lily gulped. "What if they can't?"

There was a moment's silence as they all looked at each other.

"We've got to solve this mystery!" Zara declared. "Amethyst dorm, we're going to find out who created these tornadoes and we're going to stop them!"

CHAPTER SIX

Lily and the others were settling into their seats ready for their Geography lesson, when the door opened and Ms Tulip hurried in. She taught Riding, and Lily loved her cross-country lessons.

"Girls! Boys!" She clapped her hands. "Ms Rivers has sent me to tell you there will be no Geography class today. There have been reports of another tornado sweeping through one of the villages south of the academy. The damage is very bad and Ms Nettles wants all students and their unicorns to ride there to help with the clear-up. Put your books away and go to the

stables. You will be out all day – a packed lunch will be provided for you."

She left the room and everyone began to chatter in excitement as they tidied their books away. Zara turned to the others in Amethyst dorm.

"This is our chance! We might find some clues in the damaged village that will help us to work out what's going on!"

It was a crisp winter morning. The academy buildings were covered with a layer of glittering frost and Sparkle Lake glowed like a rainbow in the pale winter sunlight. The students cantered their unicorns in a snaking line out of the grounds and towards the damaged village. Everyone carried a backpack containing an emergency repair kit of things like string, nails and a hammer, and also their lunch.

"I hope we're able to help," Feather said

worriedly, as her hooves pounded on the hard
ground.

"Me too," said Lily, wrapping her hands in
Feather's mane for warmth. "We must be nearly
there," she added. The path they were on was
covered with a fine layer of purple dust. As they
drew closer to the village, Lily gasped. There was
so much damage! Windows were smashed, doors

and roofs were missing and nothing was where it should be.

Ms Rivers pulled up, waving at the students to come together so she could address them. "Spread out," she said. "Help as many people and animals as you can but do not put yourself in any danger. If you can't solve the problem, then find a teacher and ask for help!"

"Where shall we start?" asked Feather. Her ears swivelled. "Listen!" she exclaimed. "Can you hear that?"

Lily heard it too, the whine of an animal in distress – a dog, maybe. "It's coming from over there," she said, pointing to a sheet of metal roofing lying on the ground next to a smashed-up barn. "Something's trapped underneath."

Feather picked her way over, treading a careful path through broken tiles, bricks and other debris. Lily jumped from her back and, using both hands, she tried to lift the metal up

"It's really heavy!" she puffed. Flexing her fingers, she heaved with all her might. With a grating sound, the metal moved a tiny bit. Through the gap, Lily felt the tickle of breath on her hands and heard the plaintive whining get louder. She bit her lip, holding the metal sheet steady but unable to lift it any higher. Feather used her muzzle to

Lily and Feather

try to help, but it only moved a few centimetres.

"Move, metal! Move!" Feather said, stamping a hoof in frustration. Pink sparks suddenly flew up, accompanied by the strong smell of burnt sugar.

Lily gasped. "Feather! What's happening?"

Feather didn't speak. She was staring intently at the metal sheet. It started to lift up into the air! Lily watched open-mouthed as it slowly floated to a patch of nettles and came down to rest. With a grateful woof, the dog who had been trapped under it bolted away.

"Feather! You've found your magic!" Lily cried.

"I have!" said Feather, sounding equally

surprised. "I've got moving magic, Lily. Just like my grampy."

Aisha, Zara and Phoebe came running over.

"Did Feather just move that metal sheet by magic?" Zara demanded.

"I did! I did!" Feather whinnied excitedly. "I've got moving magic!"

"Bravo, Feather, you superstar!" Phoebe gasped. "Everyone!" she shouted. "Feather's found her magic and it's amazing!"

Feather was the first unicorn in their year to get her magic. The nearby students crowded round, all wanting to congratulate her. Lily shyly stood to one side as Feather seemed to grow with the praise.

"Let's see you move something again!" said Silver.

"OK. Watch me move that chimney," said Feather, stamping a hoof and making a fallen

chimney rise into the air. Feather turned it the right way up and set it down by the side of the house it had fallen from. Everyone cheered. Feather looked delighted. "Now watch me lift up that cart."

"Shouldn't you have a rest first?" asked Lily anxiously. Her mum had warned her that when unicorns first started using their magic they usually found it very draining.

"I'm perfectly fine, thanks," said Feather airily.

"You probably shouldn't do too much at first," said Aisha in concern.

"Yes, your magic's brilliant, Feather, but you don't want to overdo it, and we should all get on with more tidying," said Zara. "You can show us more later when we're back at school."

The rest of the students nodded and hurried off, apart from Skye and Amber.

"Do something else!" Skye called.

"Yeah, let's see what else you can move!" said Amber.

Feather looked pleased. "All right."

"No, Feather, you'll tire yourself out," protested Lily.

Feather ignored her and faced the upside-down cart. She stamped her hoof. "Move, cart!" With a faint hiss, a lone pink spark rose from the ground and then faded. The cart trembled and its wheels spun.

Skye and Amber giggled.

"I wouldn't call that brilliant," said Skye.

"Move," said Feather, her cheeks wobbling with determination. She stamped a hoof again and this time two sparks flew up and a barrel lying near to the cart rose in the air.

"Eeek!" Amber shrieked, pulling Skye down just in time as the barrel swept over their heads with only a centimetre to spare, and then came

crashing down next to them, breaking into smithereens.

Skye sat up, her eyes wide. "Feather, you idiot! You could have hurt us! Your moving magic isn't brilliant, it's rubbish!" She pointed scornfully at the barrel. "And you're useless at it!"

Feather's face fell and she glanced hopefully at Lily.

Lily knew that she should defend Feather but she was too scared of what Skye might say to her if she did and the words got tangled on her tongue.

Skye and Amber walked away.

"Take no notice of them, Feather!" Lily said quickly. "Your magic is great." Her heart sank as she saw the hurt look on her unicorn's face. She knew Feather felt she'd let her down.

"Feather?" she said falteringly. But Feather just walked away.

CHAPTER SEVEN

A huge silence yawned between Lily and Feather as they rode back to school. Lily felt awful. Why hadn't she defended Feather to Skye?

Because you're a coward, a voice whispered in her head. *If you can't even stand up for your own unicorn, you'll never be brave enough to be a guardian!*

When they got back to the stables, Lily fluffed up the fresh straw in Feather's stall and brought her an extra-large helping of sky berries, the magical fruit that helped to replenish a unicorn's magic. She acted as though everything was fine, hoping that if she pretended things were normal

between her and Feather they would be.

"Lots of yummy sky berries. You'll feel stronger after eating these," said Lily, tipping the berries into Feather's manger.

"Thanks," Feather muttered.

Lily went to the door and then hesitated. Part of her just wanted to leave the stable, to say goodnight and hurry inside. But she couldn't keep pretending that everything was OK when she knew that it wasn't. Gathering her courage, she forced herself to speak. "Feather, I'm so sorry," she said. "I should have stood up to Skye. I wanted to. I really did. But I couldn't get my words out."

Feather nodded stiffly. "OK… Well, thanks for apologising but I think I'll rest now. I am rather tired," she said, turning her back on Lily.

"See you tomorrow then," Lily whispered unhappily, leaving the stable.

She was walking slowly back to the academy when someone ran up behind her.

"Lily, wait," said Aisha, slipping her arm through Lily's. "I couldn't help overhearing some of the stuff back there, in the stables with Feather. Are you all right?"

"Not really. I think I've completely messed things up between Feather and me," said Lily miserably.

"Don't worry, I'm sure it can be fixed," Aisha reassured her. She thought for a moment. "I know! Why don't you go to the stables early tomorrow and offer to help Feather practise her magic? I practise playing my flute every day. I bet Feather will get really good at using her moving magic once she's practised a bit more, and she'll be happy if you offer to help her."

That makes sense. It's like my paper folding, thought Lily. She'd been useless at it to start with but with

lots of practice her paper models were now quite good. "That's a great idea. Thanks, Aisha. I'll go and see Feather first thing and ask if she wants my help."

"I bet she'll say yes!" said Aisha. "And everything will be OK again!" The two girls shared a hopeful smile.

Lily woke up early the following morning before the sun had started to rise. Quietly, she dressed in the dark room. She took a torch from her drawer, and then picked up the paper unicorn she had made before she went to bed and slipped outside to the stables. The icy January air stung her cheeks as she ran along the path.

When she got to the stables, she found Feather asleep, curled up in the straw, her nostrils quivering and her long eyelashes fluttering on her face. Lily stood for a moment, her heart swelling with love.

I won't let you down again, Feather. I'll be braver from now on. I'll stand up for you, no matter how scared I am, Lily silently promised.

Feather woke suddenly, her eyes snapping open. She jumped up. "Lily! What are you doing here so early?"

"I wanted to say sorry again. I'm going to stand up for you in future, and not let anyone put you down – ever!" Lily said in a rush. "Look, I made you this and I came to help you practise your magic – if you want my help…" She stopped,

suddenly shy of Feather's reaction. Timidly, she placed the paper unicorn on Feather's manger.

"Did you really make this?" Feather asked, gently touching the delicate unicorn with her nose. "You're so clever, Lily."

"It was nothing," said Lily, and then she added truthfully, "Actually, it wasn't nothing. It was really hard and I had to practise for ages before I got it right but I did it and now I want you to have it."

Feather studied her for a moment. "Thank you. Yesterday was awful. I felt really stupid when you didn't stand up for me. But I thought about it last night and I realised how difficult it must have been for you when Skye was being mean. I felt glad you'd said sorry afterwards and I wish I'd said something nicer back." She pushed her head against Lily. "I couldn't get to sleep for ages. I just wanted us to make up. I don't want anything to come between us ever again."

Lily and Feather

"Me neither," said Lily with feeling. "I really *am* sorry and I promise I will always be there for you from now on."

"And I'll be there for you," Feather vowed.

They hugged each other tightly.

"So, do you want to practise some magic?" Lily asked.

Feather nodded eagerly. She started by moving small things, a hoof pick, a grooming brush, then a comb, lifting them up and bringing them to Lily. After a while, she tried bigger things like a bucket, empty at first and then one filled with water. She was soon very good at it. After that, Feather started to have some fun.

"Is that Skye's hoodie?" Lily giggled as Feather hung the forgotten hoodie from a rafter. "Feather, that's Dynamo's rug, put it back!" she added as Feather draped a striped orange rug across an empty stall to make a tent. Feather was decorating

the clock hands with ribbons she'd moved from the store room when Aisha came in, making Lily and her both jump.

"Eeek! You scared me! I usually hear you humming before you arrive," said Lily, clutching her heart and giggling.

"I can hum if you want. I just didn't want to wake anyone up," said Aisha with a grin. "I saw you'd gone from the dorm and thought I'd find you here. Are you coming in for breakfast?"

"I could use my magic and you could both have breakfast here," said Feather, her eyes shining. "We could get Silver and have a picnic in the barn next to the stables. What would you like to eat?"

"Ooh, that'd be fun. I'll have scrambled eggs, toast and apple juice please," said Aisha.

"That sounds nice. Can I have the same?" Lily asked.

Lily and Feather

Aisha went to get Silver and they all made their way to the barn. While Lily and Aisha arranged some hay bales to sit on, Feather used her moving magic to bring them food from the kitchen and sky berries from the feed room.

"Wow, look!" Aisha giggled and clutched hold of Lily as plates of scrambled egg, a rack of toast, a jug of apple juice, glasses and cutlery floated through the open barn door, followed by two buckets of sky berries.

Silver whinnied in appreciation. "I wish I had moving magic!"

"Feather, you're just showing off now!" Lily said with a grin as Feather made a knife and fork bow to each other before performing a lively dance.

"Never!" Feather said, wide-eyed as she made the spoons turn somersaults.

"This is the best way to have breakfast," said Aisha as they settled down to eat.

"Isn't it just?" Lily sighed with contentment as she looked at Aisha, Silver and Feather. For the first time since starting at Unicorn Academy, she actually felt as if she really and truly belonged there.

Lily and Feather

They were just finishing when they heard the drum of hooves on hard winter ground. "What's that?" said Silver.

They went to the barn door. A group of unicorns and adult riders were galloping away from the stables across the school grounds.

"That's the teachers!" exclaimed Lily. "Where are they off to?"

"It must be something urgent, the speed they're going," said Aisha.

"Maybe it's something to do with the tornadoes?" said Feather anxiously.

Aisha grabbed Lily's hand. "Quick, let's go and find out what's going on. See you later, Silver!"

Lily blew Feather a kiss and then she and Aisha raced back to school.

CHAPTER EIGHT

An eerie quiet hung over the academy. The corridors were unusually deserted of students and staff. The Amethyst dormitory was empty when Lily and Aisha went looking for Zara and Phoebe. They found them in the lounge, huddled beside a roaring fire. Zara was writing furiously in her notebook and Phoebe was pacing up and down.

"What's happened?" asked Aisha.

"Devastation! Chaos!" said Phoebe with a dramatic sweep of her arm. "Our beautiful island is being destroyed by purple tornadoes. They're whirling across the land, destroying everything in

their path!"

"Enough with the drama, Phoebs," said Zara. Pushing her hair behind her ears, she explained. "There have been lots more purple tornadoes in the night, closer to the school. The teachers have gone to investigate. I overheard Ms Nettles discussing it with Ms Rosemary. They're convinced it's someone using dark magic."

"But why didn't they take us with them to help clear up?" said Aisha.

"They're worried that another tornado will hit nearby while they're out and they thought we'd be safer here at school."

Lily caught her breath. "But what if a tornado hits the academy?" They all looked at her. She rushed on. "I told you what I'd seen on the map. It looked like the tornadoes are zigzagging across the island and if they keep going, they'll reach the school! The teachers mustn't have realised!"

"Let's go and check!" cried Zara.

They raced to the hall. The force field protecting the map stopped humming and let them through straight away.

It's as if it wants us to help, Lily thought. She hurried closer and her heart sank as she saw how damaged the map was now. A line of destruction criss-crossed the island.

"You're right, Lily!" Zara breathed, pointing. "If the tornadoes carry on at the same trajectory and same pace, it looks like one will hit the school today!"

"What should we do?" Aisha's eyes were huge. "The teachers have all gone!"

"We're going to die!" exclaimed Phoebe.

"We need to warn everyone," said Zara. "There's still time for us to evacuate."

"But what about the academy?" Lily couldn't bear the thought of it being smashed to pieces,

destroyed like the village they had been to. "There has to be a way we can save it!"

"There's nothing we can do," said Phoebe. "None of our unicorns have magic yet, except Feather."

Feather! A daring plan sprang into Lily's brain. She bit her lip. Should she say it out loud? Would her friends just laugh at her? She shoved her fears down. She'd decided she was going to speak up from now on and she would start right away!

"Feather might be able to help!" she burst out. "She could try to use her moving magic to steer the tornado away from the school and push it out to sea where it won't harm anything else."

"Oh, yes!" Phoebe cried, clasping her hands, and Aisha nodded.

Zara frowned. "Lily, I really don't mean this to sound horrible but is Feather's magic strong enough to do something like that yet?"

"She was awesome this morning!" said Aisha. "She was moving whatever she wanted."

Lily shot her a grateful look. "Look, it may not work," she said to Zara. "I can't promise she'll be able to do it but I believe in her, and, right now, we haven't got any other plan. This might be our only hope! We've got to try!"

"Right then," said Zara, taking command. "If you believe Feather can do it, then I believe it too, Lily." Lily glowed inside. "Let's call a meeting of the whole

school in the stables and Lily can tell everyone what the plan is."

Lily paled at Zara's words. It was one thing speaking in front of her friends but the whole school? "Oh no!" she whispered, shaking her head. "I can't speak in front of everyone. I just can't. Please can you do that part, Zara?"

"If you're sure?" Zara looked pleased when Lily nodded. "Right then. I'll do that bit. You go and tell Feather what's happening and we'll get everyone to the stables! Come on! There isn't a moment to waste!"

As Lily ran to the stables, she felt a curl of panic inside. Should she have asked Feather before offering her help? But there hadn't been time. She ran faster, needing to explain to Feather before everyone descended on her.

"Lily, what is it?" Feather left her hay as Lily ran into her stall.

Panting for breath, Lily explained.

For a moment, Feather was silent, then she asked tentatively, "Do you think I can do this, Lily? Do you really believe my magic is strong enough?"

Lily didn't hesitate. "Yes. I do. You can help save the school, Feather. I know it."

Feather took a deep breath. "Then I'll try."

"I'll be with you the whole time." Lily suddenly felt very fierce. "And if anyone dares say anything mean, they'll have me to deal with!"

The students all gathered in the stable yard, shouting and calling out, wanting to know what was going on. Zara stood on a mounting block and addressed them. "Listen up, everyone," she called, clapping her hands like a teacher. "This is an emergency."

She quickly explained about the tornado and

how Feather was going to try to stop it. She'd barely finished speaking when Skye started to sneer.

"As if that will work," she scoffed. "Feather's magic isn't strong enough to move a cart let alone a supernatural tornado!"

"Oh, yes it is!" cried Lily. Feather gave her a grateful look. "Feather was tired yesterday because she'd only just got her magic but she's been practising this morning and she's really good at using it now. So you can just … just *shut up*, Skye!"

There were a number of gasps. Skye gaped, lost for words for once. Feather nuzzled Lily's shoulder and she felt a happy glow spread through her.

"Lily's right," called Aisha. "Feather can do this."

Silver whinnied in support and the rest of the unicorns joined in.

"She can!" cried Lily. "I believe in her!"

Skye found her voice again. "Oh, well, that's all right then – Lily believes in Feather. What could there possibly be to worry about?" Her voice was sarcastic.

Feather stamped her foot angrily. "Enough, Skye!" A spark shot up from her hoof as she stared at a bucket of water beside the mounting block. It rose into the air and floated to a point above Skye's head.

The other students noticed and started to gasp and point. Skye looked up. As she did so the bucket slowly started to tip.

"No!" shrieked Skye, realising the water was about to drop on top of her. She leapt out of the way but the bucket followed her. A few water droplets landed on Skye's head as the bucket floated above her.

Lily bit back her grin. "I'm sure Feather can

prove to you how good her magic is, Skye."

"What? Like this, you mean, Lily?" said Feather.

The bucket tipped slightly more and a few more drops splashed out.

Everyone giggled as Skye jumped around trying to avoid the water.

"Stop!" she said, gasping. "Please, stop, Feather!"

"Are you with us then?" asked Lily.

"Yes," mumbled Skye.

"Sorry, I didn't quite catch that," said Lily, starting to enjoy herself.

"YES! I believe Feather can do magic. OK?" Skye cried angrily.

Lily felt a rush of triumph as Feather moved the bucket and set it down on the ground. "Then what are we waiting for?" she shouted, courage rushing through her as she saw the look of love that Feather was sending her. "Let's save the school!"

CHAPTER NINE

As everyone cleared a space around Feather, Aisha let out a squeal. "Lily, your hair! You've bonded with Feather."

Lily lifted the violet, yellow and blue strand in her black hair and stared at it in wonder.

Feather nuzzled her face against Lily's.

"Three cheers for Lily and Feather! The first partners at Unicorn Academy to find their magic and bond! Hip, hip, hooray!" Phoebe cried.

As the cheering died away the sky suddenly darkened and a breeze sprang up from nowhere, sending empty buckets clattering across the yard.

"It's the tornado!" said Zara. "It's coming! Into the stable block, everyone, where it's safe!"

Lily took a deep breath as the others started hurrying inside. "This is it, Feather."

Feather lifted her head. "I'm going to save the academy, Lily!"

Lily placed a hand on her neck. "And I'm going to be right here with you."

The wind grew fiercer, tossing Lily's hair and Feather's mane around. There was a roaring noise that quickly grew louder. In the distance, Lily saw a blur of purple coming across the grounds towards the school buildings. The trees began to bend, their branches whipping back and forth. Twigs snapped off and twirled in the air. Lily, standing shoulder to shoulder with Feather, ducked to avoid the flying debris as bits of trees and bushes whirled past her and the wind screamed in her ears.

Lily and Feather

The tornado grew, towering in the air as it headed towards the academy like an enormous shadowy building. It glittered dully as it spun closer, depositing a grimy layer of purple dust over the grounds and into Sparkle Lake. The stench of bad magic hung in the air. It tickled the back of Lily's throat, making her cough and her eyes water.

Feather, her gaze fixed on the tornado, repeatedly muttered, "I can do this."

"You can!" Lily said hoarsely. "I know you can!" She wiped her streaming eyes. The tornado was so close – any minute now it would hit them… Lily blinked. The tornado looked like it was hesitating. Was it turning away from the school or was that wishful thinking? No, it was definitely moving, gradually changing course, heading towards the mountains and slowly rising over them and out to sea. "It's working!" she cried, stroking Feather's neck. "Don't give up, Feather."

Lily *and* Feather

"Stay beside me, Lily," Feather panted. "Keep talking to me. It helps."

"I'm not going anywhere." Lily continued to stroke Feather's straining neck as she focused her magic to move the tornado. "I know you're strong enough to do this."

The tornado moved even further away. "It's almost gone!" she exclaimed. "Keep going, Feather."

The towering purple tornado rose over the highest mountain peak, wobbling as it moved away. Then suddenly a man's voice boomed from the sky. His words were strong at first but faded away as the tornado banked to the west and spun out to sea. "You think you can stop me but you can't. I will…"

His voice faded into howling wind.

Feather's body trembled and her legs sagged.

"You did it, Feather!" Lily cried.

Zara, Phoebe and Aisha ran out of the stable block.

"Did you hear that man's voice?" asked Zara, pulling out her notebook. "What did it say? 'You think you can stop me but you can't…' What else did he say?"

Everyone shook their heads. No one had heard the rest of the words.

"I've no idea what this means," said Zara, her mouth set in a determined line, "but at least we know now that the person behind these tornadoes is a man. I'm going to find out more!"

"We'll all help, won't we?" said Aisha. "If we don't find out who did this, they could do it again! Raise your hand if you're in."

Lily, Zara, Phoebe and Aisha all raised their hands, slapping their palms together as they made

their pact.

"Amethyst dorm will find the culprit!" chanted Phoebe. "Amethyst dorm is the best!"

Everyone else started to spill out of the stable block and at the same moment Lily heard the sound of beating hooves.

"It's the teachers!" she said, spinning round to look.

Ms Nettles, closely followed by the rest of the staff, galloped up.

"Is everyone all right?" Ms Nettles demanded. "What happened? We saw the tornado heading towards the school and we came back as fast as we could. Where did it go?"

All eyes turned to Lily and Feather, and Lily felt her face flood with colour. Feather nodded as if to say, "You can do this." Lily took a deep breath but as she started to speak Skye stepped forward.

"We were all indoors when—"

"Be quiet, Skye," said Zara.

"Let Lily and Feather speak if they want to; it's their story," Aisha said.

Lily smiled gratefully at her new friends. She paused for another moment, then poured out the story.

Ms Nettles listened carefully, her glasses rattling as Lily retold their adventures, from tracking the storm on the magic map to Feather's heroism in stopping it.

"Thank you for saving the academy, Feather, and to you, Lily, for encouraging her and standing with her. If you hadn't been there for her, her magic wouldn't have been strong enough. It's the bond between a unicorn and their partner that gives the unicorn's magic added power and strength," said Ms Nettles. "I'm delighted you have bonded and discovered Feather's magic. I told you the other day that guardians all have

different strengths – well, the one quality all guardians share is bravery, and you have certainly shown that today."

"I – I'm not brave," stammered Lily.

Ms Nettles' eyes seemed to see right inside her. "You are, my dear. Bravery is not about who shouts the loudest, it's about doing what you know is right even when that's difficult and you feel scared. You and Feather are truly brave, Lily, and I know you will be wonderful guardians of our island." She smiled at them and then looked round at everyone else. "Well, this has certainly been an eventful start to the year! Now, please would everyone settle their unicorns back in the stalls then go to the hall where I'll ask Cook to provide hot chocolate and cookies."

"But, Ms Nettles, what about the person we heard?" said Zara. "Are you going to try to find out who he is?"

"Yes, after all, he may strike again!" exclaimed Phoebe.

Ms Nettles looked at them over the top of her glasses. "I understand your concern, girls, but you need not worry. The teachers and I will deal with it from now on." She turned and rode away, leaving Zara staring after her.

"We'll see about that," she muttered. "This is a mystery and I'm going to help solve it."

"We all are!" said Phoebe, linking arms with her.

"We definitely will, but, first, cookies and hot chocolate sound good, don't they, Lily?" said Aisha.

Lily grinned at her dorm – her new best friends. "Oh, yes!"

They all took their unicorns back to their stalls.

"You were brilliant," said Lily, stroking Feather's face.

Lily and Feather

"You were amazing too," said Feather, nuzzling her. "Thank you for standing up for me when Skye was being mean."

"You didn't exactly need my help!" said Lily with a grin. "Did you see Skye's face when that bucket was hanging over her head? That was very funny, Feather!" She hugged her. "I promise I'll always be here for you. I'm not going to be a shy little mouse any more and I'm going to speak out when I need to. After today, I'm not scared of anyone."

Feather whickered softly. "Me neither. We've always got each other. That's all that matters."

"It really is," said Lily, kissing her.

Feather's eyes sparkled. "But now it's time to join your friends for hot chocolate and cookies. Hold on tight, Lily." She stamped her hoof and Lily gasped as she suddenly found herself on Feather's back, gliding out of the stables and across the

grass to the school.

"Feather!" she shrieked. "What are you doing?"

"Having fun with my magic, Lily!" Feather whinnied back. "Having fun!"

AT SUNSHINE STABLES PONY CAMP, DREAMS BECOME ADVENTURES!

SUNSHINE
STABLES

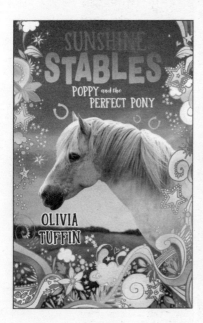

Another MAGICAL series from Nosy Crow!

SNOW SISTERS

ASTRID FOSS

THE SILVER SECRET

ASTRID FOSS

THE CRYSTAL ROSE

ASTRID FOSS

THE FROZEN RAINBOW

ASTRID FOSS

THE ENCHANTED WATERFALL